Tuesday Night Requiem

by L.S. Collison

Episode #5

Nurse Kit Carson's Knife & Gun Club Adventures

America's New Wild West

Cover Art, *Requiem*. Oil on wood by Gregory Block, 2020
Cover Design by M.G. Manelis

ISBN: 978-1-7322290-5-1 (electronic)
ISBN: 978-1-7322290-6-8 (paperback)
Copyright ©2021 by Linda Collison
Fiction House, Ltd.
Steamboat Springs, Colorado

Tuesday Night Requiem

by L.S. Collison

In a rented room at the 4Aces, a seen-better-days motel that sheltered East Colfax drifters, drovers, and drug addicts, the man who called himself the Lone Gunman stood before the bathroom mirror, armed with a toothbrush. His mama had always urged him to take care of his teeth. *Brush and floss religiously, Willie. Take good care of your teeth, and don't take up smoking, methamphetamines or cocaine, you'll ruin those pearly whites.* His beloved mama, God rest her soul, had been a dental assistant, the best damn dental hygienist in High Plains. She had also urged him to be a good boy Willie, and never play with guns. He took that advice very seriously; he never *played* with guns; he took them very seriously. Guns were his livelihood, and today he was going to make a killing.

After a final rinse and spit, Willie wiped his mouth with the white terrycloth

motel towel and admired his reflection. His lean cheeks and square jawline sported

a two-day growth of salt-and-pepper hair – the stubble was a desirable look for

High Plains cowboys. He lifted the black silk bandanna so that it rested across the

bridge of his nose, covering his lower face and neck. Adjusting the brim of the

black felt cowboy hat forward so that it hid his receding hairline and cast a shadow

over his eyes, he scrutinized his image. Yepper, a fair enough facsimile.

He wasn't the real Lone Gunman, that myth, that legend, that Western

metaphor for Death, but he had cultivated a true aim and abandoned his conscience

somewhere along the trail, traits he thought suited him for the job. Like the Grim

Reaper himself, the Lone Gunman was feared yet ignored. Folks didn't talk about

the Lone Gunman; it was better to pretend you didn't see him standing there alone,

all hangdog off to the side, like a boy at a square dance without a partner.

The way Willie saw it, the Lone Gunman was Death's own angel. Tonight, his

target, the sick nurse named Kit Carson, would go to her just reward. She'd

probably thank him, if she could. And he would be well compensated for it. But

even when he didn't have a paying job, the Lone Gunman kept his skills honed by

picking off the old and the weak, lungers and coughers who spread their germs and

sucked in more than their share of the allocated breath of life. Looking at it scientifically, he filled an ecological niche. Back before antibiotics were developed, pneumonia was deemed "the old man's friend." Inflammation of the lungs took old folks after a bout of the grippe or a fall and a broken hip. It finished them off, humanely, some would say. Pneumonia could be a blessing in disguise for those who had reached the end of their skein of existence. People clamored for "life support," not realizing they were already receiving life support – the best modern science had to offer. Today there were cures and vaccines for every damn little thing. There was no rest for the weary.

The way he saw it, what he did, he did in the name of love. There, by the door, his chosen instrument – a bolt action Springfield .30-06 – fine piece of Americana. His heirloom was in immaculate condition – cleaned, oiled, rubbed to a sheen and ready to do the master's bidding. None of those automatic slaughter machines for him. They were for pussies who shot up schools and shopping malls. The Lone Gunman had a reputation for selectivity. With his precision, his steady hand, he might have been a sniper or a surgeon. With his passion, his keen perception, his sense of timing, he might have been an artist or a musician.

The merciful assassin checked his pocket watch. The mission depended on precise timing; he needed to enter the facility during the change of shift. A tingling in his blood. It was time.

One last glance in the mirror. He pulled down the bandanna and drew back his lips in a skeletal, rictus grin – his teeth, big, white, and even as a picket fence. American teeth. Mama would be proud. He would bequeath them to the High Plains Dental Institute in her honor. The image of his own grinning skull mounted on the wall like a trophy, the image gave him a comforting sense of immortality.

Wyatt

"Wyatt, are we going to have a funeral?" His little sister, breaking through the soundproof booth inside his mind. The boy's heart froze. *She knew.* His tongue lay heavy in his mouth. Someone had told her, she guessed it, or maybe she dreamt it. Calamity was always talking about her dreams.

"Are we, Wyatt?"

He could not think of what to say. He could not even think about it, much less speak of it. "Stop talking so much; I'm trying to concentrate." His thumbs moved like lightning across the buttons of the controller.

"But we have to have a funeral. Abuela found my poor dead Hammie in the freezer, inside your sock, and she was going to put him in the trash, but I said no because Mommy said we would bury Hammie under the cottonwood trees in the summertime, after a rainstorm, when the ground is soft. Mommy promised we'd have a funeral, a celebration of his life. She said I could pad a shoebox with cottonwood seeds and sing Happy Trails. She said I could borrow her black bandanna for a pall. What's a pall, Wyatt?

He shrugged. "Ask Abuela."

"OK, but we have to wait for Mommy to get well and come back home. We can't have a funeral without Mommy."

"Sure, we'll wait for her." He felt a breath of relief rush out of his body. This was all about the fucking hamster that had died months ago. If Calamity believed Mom was going to get well, maybe there was still hope. He wanted to believe but dared not, lest he be crushed. He wanted to save her. There must be something he could do. But what? Onscreen, his avatar took a direct hit and disappeared in a puff of simulated smoke.

The video game no longer gave him pleasure. He was fidgety, like a bronc in a holding pen. It wasn't only his mother's illness that made him restless; there was something else, a feeling that he was missing out on his own life, held captive inside this crowded house. Stay inside, Wyatt. It's dangerous out there. Stay inside, stay safe. Well, he didn't want to stay inside anymore, and he didn't want to stay safe. He wanted to venture out, take a risk, do something different, maybe even dangerous. Something to make his blood race. It seemed to Wyatt that he had spent too much of his life indoors, surrounded by walls, by rules, protected. Mom had always warned him about the bad people out there. *Lock the door, don't answer it, do your homework, watch your sister.* Meanwhile, Mom went out and did battle with the world, night after night, and look what that got her--it got her sick, maybe even killed. Now it was his turn. He was old enough to have some hair on his balls. That made him a man, right? Or very nearly so. And what was he going to do with his life? Be a video game champion? No, that was just killing time. Practice. For the real thing, which Old Man Henderson next door always said was coming.

Later that afternoon...

"Come on, Mike. Let's go."

"Where to, Wyatt?"

"Downtown. Balmy's on the Three-Ten to High Plains. You want to come along?"

"Sure."

An adventure was no good if it wasn't shared. His best friend, Mike Trujillo, was his only friend. A whole year younger than Wyatt, Mike knew so much more about High Plains street life, having lived in homeless camps for some months before his family took shelter in the back of Kit's truck and soon after found their way inside the Carson's home. Now, having escaped the boring confines of the house, they were on a mission; they were going to the Trailways station to meet

Balmy, who was on her way down from Indian Country where she had been hiding out with sister Stormy under the protection of the Arapahoe and the Shoshone.

Wyatt took a handful of coins from the Mason jar on his mother's dresser. He thought about taking the Glock from under his bed, but the piece was too big. Too obvious. Besides, it was the house weapon -- meant to kill home intruders and for that reason should stay in the home. Instead, he chose the Smith & Wesson seven-shooter, an antique pocket pistol from the family heirloom case, and loaded it with the accompanying .22 black powder cartridges. Fact: Samuel Clemens had carried one of these on his travels out West, he bragged to Mike. Yeah, Mark fucking Twain. It doesn't get more American than that.

"Do you really want to walk around with a loaded antique gun in your pants pocket?" Personally, Mike preferred to carry a folding knife his uncle had given him.

But Wyatt had read Samuel Clemens's article "Advice to Youth" in which the great writer warns of the danger of unloaded firearms. Said the wag, *They are the most deadly and unerring things that have ever been created by man. You don't have to have any sights on the gun, you don't have to take aim, even. No, you just pick out a relative and bang away, and you are sure to get him. A youth who can't hit a cathedral at thirty yards with a Gatling gun in three-quarters of an hour, can take up an old empty musket and bag his mother every time at a hundred.*

The irony and sarcasm went over Wyatt's juvenile head. His heart pounded, but not with fear. Not exactly. It felt more like excitement. And what was the difference between fear and excitement? He aimed to find out.

The two boys walked through the neighborhoods – Mexican, Italian, Hungarian – cutting through the alleyways toward the bottomland where the tracks ran, where the small population of Chinese had set up their laundries, their restaurants, their drug dens, right alongside the poorer sort of billiard rooms, brothels, and Irish grog shops. Red paper lanterns hanging over the street, there seemed to be some kind of festival going on – vendors selling white dumplings from street carts and the pop- pop of firecrackers in the allies. Gang tags everywhere. Waddies, Toros, Tongs, Latin Kings. Mike knew which group had made which signs, or at least he claimed to know. "We don't want to be here after dark, Wyatt."

Wyatt was aware of the weapon, felt it solid against his thigh with every step. They bought two bottles of Fanta at an immigrant convenience store, guzzled them down in the shade cast on the east side of the building. Late afternoon, still hot, it would stay light a long, long time. Summer days were endless.

A man lying on the sidewalk, next to a buggy piled high with supplies. Was he sleeping, or was he dead? People walked right past him, like he wasn't even there. Wyatt guessed he was passed out drunk or overdosed. Should he call for help? Why wasn't anyone else doing anything? He knew what his mother would do. Wyatt touched 9-1-1 on his keypad.

"There's a man down on the sidewalk, Fifteenth and Wazee. I don't know what's wrong. I think he might need some help."

Minutes later, flashing lights. Wyatt wanted to stay and watch but the lawman said, "You kids run along. Git on home, go on." Mike pulled at his sleeve, anxious to keep moving. The Law made him nervous.

Hearing the crack of pool balls, they stopped at a basement saloon, beneath the Oriental Palace: Poolhall, Saloon and Chinese Take-Out, the sign advertised. Six feet under the main floor of the hotel, cool and dark as a grave, lit only by flickering neon beer signs. The clink of glasses, the easy talk of men. A whiff of whiskey and a hint of sewer gas. Wyatt watched the men rack 'em up three times, watching carefully, seeing how the game was played. A Chinese kid, a boy about Wyatt's own age; it was hard to tell. Name of Zhang. Said he worked there. Ran errands for customers, delivered food, pushed a broom, and brushed the felt tops of the billiard tables. Wyatt envied him his freedom. Working meant money and

money meant freedom. At least to Wyatt it did.

"Want to play?"

"Does it cost money?"

Zhang grinned. "Depends."

"On what?"

"On whether you win or lose."

"I don't have any money."

"Do you have anything to put up? Anything of value?

Wyatt felt the weight of the pistol deep in his pocket.

"Yeah."

"Let's see it."

He withdrew the antique revolver, opening his fingers to reveal it, like a choice

crabapple.

Zhang nodded approvingly. "That's a nice little piece. Does it actually fire?"

"I wouldn't carry it if it didn't. And yeah, it's loaded." But he wasn't certain if it

would actually fire, the black powder cartridges were so old.

"What do you have to put up, Zhang?" Mike, looking after his friend's interest.

"Joss."

"What's that?"

"It's money. Not the kind you spend here on Earth."

"Who wants that?"

"The ghosts of our ancestors."

Wyatt laughed. "How can they spend it if they're dead? You can't take it with you."

Zhang shrugged. "Maybe you can. We burn it for them, and it goes up in smoke."

Wyatt felt a breath of cold air touch the back of his neck. "Well, I don't believe in ghosts. What else you got?"

Zhang chewed his lip as he considered the question, then pulled a plastic bag out of his pocket. It held a wad of something gray, maybe some kind of drug, or maybe it was a rhino's balls, or some weird Chinese herb. Wyatt didn't want to reveal his ignorance.

"I changed my mind. I don't want to put up my piece."

"Then you shouldn't have pulled it out of your pants, cowboy." Zhang grinned, breaking the tension. "Hey, look, I'll play you cowboys one game, just for the hell of it. No bets. But next time, bring silver, OK? More fun that way." He handed them cue sticks from the rack on the wall and a cube of chalk from his pocket. The boys chalked the tips of their sticks as they had seen the other players do.

"Go ahead. You break 'em," Zhang said.

Wyatt racked the balls, then placed the cue ball where the others had, carefully lining up his shot. Just then his cell phone pinged with an incoming text. It was Balmy, at the station. Shooting pool would have to wait.

Balmy Wether

Moms real sick, maybe dyin, I thought you should know.

Reading Wyatt's text, her gut twisted, and she had answered impulsively.

Im on my way.

It was dangerous, but Balmy had been planning to go back to High Plains anyway, to meet with Polly Pry, the outlaw reporter from the Rocky Mountain Gazette. Pry had brought down more than one political career since coming to the territory. The last reporter, the back-east dude who interviewed Stormy after the shootout on the border of Wyoming, that reporter had been fired, or maybe even shot. In any case, the story had been killed, that much was apparent. Buried somewhere deep in the back pages with the unimportant news, the happenings no one ever read, or shared, or tweeted, or gave a shit about. Ratzer's campaign posse probably saw to that.

But Balmy Wether had yet to tell her own story, a bigger story than the breach of some two-bit nondisclosure agreement between a pole dancer and a political pimp. She had been following Polly Pry on social media. Now she messaged her and arranged a meeting to expose Bully Ratzer. The timing was perfect, with the election only a few months away. This time the story would not be killed; she would see to that. And now going to High Plains was even more imperative. Nurse Kit Carson was real sick, Wyatt had said.

The next day, Balmy was at the bus stop in Riverton, ticket in hand, purchased with the money she made waiting tables at the café. Dressed in baggy, secondhand sweats and cheap running shoes, she thought she might pass for a boy. Her scalp stung from a dozen nicks and cuts. She had shaved her own head so she wouldn't be recognized by Ratzer's men, who were everywhere in High Plains. Balmy's long dark hair, arrow straight and shiny as a crow's feather, had been a hallmark of hers when she danced. Hair down to the bottom of her butt. Now that it was shaved off, she felt light. Much cooler. Less burdened. Stronger, somehow. It felt like the opposite of Samson, was it Samson? Samson and Delilah, yeah. Balmy's hair had been her weakness, and now that she had cut it off, she felt liberated. Her hair was history – she had been released from her past.

Traveling light, all she owned in a pillowcase. Everyone else on the motor coach was packing heat, but all she had for a weapon was a pointed nail file. And no hair to hide behind. At least she did have a smartphone. Information was power, information could be used as a weapon, although it was slower than a bullet or the thrust of a knife. Unlike bullets, information was unlimited, with a smartphone or a computer you would never run out. She was still unsure about which information was reliable and which was bullshit, but she was learning. Having just earned her G.E.D. online, Balmy had enrolled in online classes at Arapaho Community College. She wanted to be a journalist. She wanted to expose all the injustice in the world, starting with Sheriff Bully Ratzer.

Now that Stormy was safe with the Indians, working at the casino under a new name, Balmy could get on with her life. She had never wanted to be a sex worker. What young girl dreams of being a lap dancer when she grows up? Unlike Stormy, who claimed her great-great grandmother was full blooded Shoshone, Balmy could prove no tribal affiliation. In truth, she didn't know who she was or where she had come from. She had blended genetic traits, being the eye-pleasing product of mixed-race parentage, a slightly exotic look, with dark, wideset eyes and a dusky hue to her flawless skin. But her past was a blank slate. She had no memories of a mother, much less a father. No roots to ground her. Balmy was a free bird. And that called for a new name. She was no longer half of the Stormy and Balmy

Wether Sisters act. Stormy might have signed a nondisclosure with Ratzer but

Balmy hadn't. At fifteen, she hadn't been old enough to sign a legal document. She

still wasn't "legal" in that sense, which made Ratzer's crime all the worse. Sex

trafficking of minors. It was bad enough he was a crooked sheriff, abusing his

position, making money from criminal activities, but she hated herself for having

done his bidding. There was no amount of money that would take that shame away.

She would expose him, she would bring him down, she would end his political

aspirations and, in the process, kick-start her own career in investigative

journalism.

But poor Wyatt and sweet little Calamity. Balmy's heart tightened thinking

about them. She felt a duty to help them and to help Kit, the nurse who had risked

her life for her and sheltered her after what happened to Stormy.

The Trailways coach slowed as it prepared to pull into the station. Her phone

said 3:10. She texted Polly Pry, *Arrived.* The reporter texted back, *Meet me at the*

Oriental.

Looking up from her phone, Balmy caught a glimpse of a black town car with

tinted windows parked across the street. Nervous, she ran a hand across her bare

head. *Relax. Could be any pimp's ride.* As the bus braked to its final stop, she fired off a text to Tonto to let him know of her arrival. She would need some backup. Especially when the dirt she had on Ratzer hit the wind.

Tonto

When he received Balmy's text, Tim Rhodes had just activated his phone after three days of being off the grid. Immediately, the screen filled with urgent messages.

The man known as Tonto was on his way back from the Arapaho Sundance, having gone to find an herb, a berry, a bark, a root – some authentic healing concoction or decoction, something to cure Kit, to rid her of the grippe. And peyote, he had gone for that too. For the insight, the greater vision, it might bring. He regretted having waited so long in life to embrace his Arapaho blood. Western medicine was failing him, it was failing everyone. The scientific process was being subverted by profit, by corporate greed. The basis of Western Medicine was science based, and the basis of Western hospitals was professional nursing care, and both had been subverted. The answer, his answer, was to start a non-profit hospital owned and operated by nurses. A co-op organization, like a credit union.

Tonto stopped just north of Fort Collins to relieve himself and to reconnect with the wider world. Turned his cellphone on and discovered the shit had hit the fan again. Wellmart was in chaos. Patients' lives were in danger, including Kit's – not just from the bug but from lack of medical attention and skilled nursing care. The corporate bottom line was killing people and on top of that, Balmy Wether had left the reservation, was back in High Plains, Ratzer's goons were hell-bent on silencing his opposition and the so-called Lone Gunman was still at large, delivering deadly bullets in a random sort of fashion. Or maybe they were working together. And all he wanted to do was to start a nonprofit hospital, then retire. He was ready to enjoy the good life. Hunting, fishing, riding. Drinking a beer or smoking a joint and watching the sun go down. Watching his grandkids grow up. Which seemed unlikely, since to his knowledge, he had not fathered any children. But there were always surrogates. Blood wasn't everything. Kit had children in need of a father figure.

Richard 'Big Dick' Beamis

Help! Nurse!

He tried to make the words come out of his mouth, but they got lost somewhere in the uncharted territory of his brain. *Where in this hell was his nurse?*

Richard Beamis, the chief executive officer of Wellmart Healthcare Corporation, was a VIP patient in his own hospital's Intensive Care Unit. He had been there a week with little change in his critical, but stable, condition. There were no moves being made to transfer him home or to rehab, or even to the neuro floor. It was an awkward situation. Beamis was taking up valuable real estate – the ICU was for those who needed high level nursing care and monitoring, and the miracles of modern life support that the ICU nurses and respiratory therapists knew how to operate. They worked as a specially trained force, like the Navy SEALs, they were SWAT Nurses. As the hospital's head honcho, Beamis deserved the level of staffing available only in this elite unit. The physicians were reluctant to move him anywhere, despite pressure from the insurance company. The ailing CEO of Wellmart deserved the very best the company had to offer.

Even though the hospital ran well enough on its own, Beamis was the self-styled visionary who drove the corporation's policy of growth and acquisition, that, in turn, fueled the confidence in the market. Healthcare was big business in America, presenting limitless opportunities for growth. After all, everyone was born and everyone needed interventions throughout their lives, and in the end, everyone died. From cradle to grave, every intervention could be provided by Wellmart, the largest for-profit healthcare company in the American West. But Richard Beamis wasn't called "Big Dick" for nothing. He intended to steer the corporation to become the largest, the most profitable, in the New West. Hell, why stop there? Why not the whole world?

The main problem was, at the moment, Big Dick could not speak. Could not write.

Could not make himself understood. He knew what he wanted to say but try as he

might, he could not make the words come out. Earlier that week, when the speech

therapist came to work with him, he grasped wildly for her hand, his eyes wide. He

tried so hard to tell her, but the sound that came out of his throat meant nothing

to her. He tried to write a message, but somewhere between his brain and his one

working hand, the words got derailed. His message was a toddler's scribble.

"It's alright, Mr. Beamis. Richard. Big Dick. Can I call you that?" Her smile was

genuine. If anyone could help him learn to speak again, this highly trained and

sympathetic young therapist could. If she knew Beamis had undercut her employee

compensation package, she gave no hint of it. "Learning to speak again takes time.

We must be patient. With your good hand, point to what you want." She held a

laminated chart with cartoonish drawings on it. A glass of water. A figure

shivering. A figure sweating. A commode. Christ, he didn't need a goddamn drink of

water, and he didn't need the shitter – somebody was trying to kill him, for fuck's

sake! There was no picture of a masked man with a gun on the chart. He needed

protection. He needed to get the hell out of here, out of his own hospital! Where

was his wife? Where was his doctor? Where was his nurse? He shook his head no –

at least, he thought he was shaking his head. He no longer seemed to be able to command his muscles to do their job. How to make this pretty young woman understand? Alas, the therapy session was over. She made an entry on the chart and left, leaving him alone with his suspicions.

Beamis was sure he had seen him, the tall figure in the black duster, Springfield rifle over his shoulder, like a rogue soldier. The shooter who had been killing old people, sick folks, had been picking them off one by one, but no one paid much attention. These were not mass shootings, these crimes received no press coverage, the headlines were all income taxes, immigrants, and influenza. And now he saw him again, outside his room, the Lone Gunman! Richard pawed wildly for the nurse call bell with his working arm but could not reach it. He roared out, bellowing like a beast, an effort that triggered his heart monitor to sound its electronic alarm, but still no one came to his aid. From inside his brain, walled off and besieged like the Alamo, he heard his wounded self whisper, *My kingdom for a nurse.*

The person who entered his room looked like a nurse, dressed in scrubs, carrying a standard issue Ruger 9mm in a sexy leather holster and wearing a Wellmart ID badge that said NURSETTE. He didn't recognize her. She must be new.

"I've got something for you, Mr. Beamis." In her hands, an empty syringe.

Boots Calhoun

At last, Boots Calhoun had a crack at running this damn rodeo. Already a card-carrying member of the High Plains Cattlemen's Association, she had her sights set on the Cowgirl's Fortune 500 Club. Although Calhoun was only Acting CEO, there was a good chance the title could become permanent if Big Dick Beamis didn't fully recover. While the cerebral vascular accident – the stroke – hadn't killed the old cigar- smoking coot, it had caused massive damage, leaving Wellmart's CEO pretty much useless. As long as he was holed up in ICU, Boots was able to get in and make some deals of her own; she held the reins of the biggest medicine show in the West. But as sanctioned CEO, her control could be even bigger. Dammit, she knew how to turn a profit. The key was in the Patient Satisfaction Survey. The PiSS reports were golden. Customer satisfaction was what really mattered. Customer satisfaction meant a resort-like atmosphere. Folks wanted a vacation. They wanted Wi-Fi, flat screens, plush mattresses, saunas, a driving range, shooting range, ammo sold at the gift shop. And they wanted the administrators to have well-appointed offices, covered parking, and electric charging stations for their luxury cars. Boots knew right where to find the needed funds. As Chief Financial Officer, she knew just where to make the deep cuts that Big Dick had been too soft-hearted to make.

It started with staffing, across the board cuts, chop- chop. The grippe made it easier, what with furloughs in place to prevent the bug's spread. She had already slashed unit secretary positions and environmental service personnel by half, furloughed medical records personnel, with no intention of bringing them back. Now, for the professionals. She began by replacing the nurses with unlicensed workers. Pretty waitresses – excuse me, servers – with big white teeth and ivory handled pistols slung from their hips, nursettes who knew how to push pills with a smile, now that's what the customers wanted. Nursettes who knew how to handle a gun, could goddamn shoot straight. Sell every patient a damn wrist monitor to record their vitals. Doctors could start their own IVs, push their own intravenous medications, change their own postop dressings. And family members could sit with patients at night, they could play cards at the bedside. That's all the night nurses did anyway, she had heard from a reliable source. Nursettes and housekeepers would be hired part time and work for tips, tin badges and WE ARE HEALTHCARE HEROES tee shirts. That would inspire them to go the extra mile with a smile. Cheap labor and customer satisfaction were key to profits, continued corporate growth. The customer was always right. Give 'em what they want and charge 'em for it. And those who didn't have benefits? Fuck 'em. Let 'em work for companies big enough, profitable enough to provide health insurance. Will it sink small business? Well, duh! Mom and pop can't afford to pay healthcare for their employees, but we sure as hell can't have taxpayers foot the bill. Oh, hell no. Bigger business means better business. Wellmart Corporation is the biggest cock on the block, and Boots Calhoun held that big, fat cock in her capable hands.

Bully Ratzer

The sheriff of High Plains walked out of Wellmart like a champ, having licked the grippe, having kicked it in the balls. In truth, he had been scared when it hit, robbing him of his breath, leaving him gasping. In truth, he was still a little weak, and his fat, ruddy face beaded up with sweat under his ten-gallon hat, in the heat of high noon. But now that he knew he wasn't going to die, he could safely say the bug had been nothing more than a bad cold.

   Going to the hospital to seek treatment had been a stroke of luck, for Ratzer had accidentally discovered the whereabouts of that damned nurse, the one who had humiliated him with the enema, the one who had protected the porn sisters and who was still working to bring him down. Nurse Kit Carson was hiding out in Wellmart. Now that he knew who and where she was, the bitch was as good as dead. He would take no chances that she might recover and try to ruin his career again.

Before he could get into the vehicle, the reporters swarmed like mad cows, surrounding him, firing questions. He gave the cameras the victory sign and a winning grin.

"Sheriff Ratzer, can you give us a statement about your health?"

"Sheriff, are you still in the running for governor?"

"Sheriff, what are your plans to take down the grippe?"

"I have to say, I've never felt better. If that was the dreaded Chinaman's virus that ambushed me, I have to say I kicked its ass."

"Sheriff Ratzer, is the hospital still experiencing a shortage of protective equipment? Are the nurses and doctors properly armed?"

"Is there a cure for this damned bug yet?"

"What can you tell us about the care you received? Is it true there's a shortage of nurses and technicians?"

"There ain't no shortages, not in these parts. Wellmart is the best spa in the West. I just checked in for a little tune-up, that's all. The doctors have pronounced me fit as a fiddle, healthy as a horse, right as the rain."

Deputy Jones used his bulk to force an opening in the herd of reporters surrounding the luxury vehicle, opening the door. Ratzer plopped heavily into the back seat. The deputy closed the door and bid the driver to vamoose.

"Home, *Jefe?*" the driver asked.

"Not just yet. I need to make a little detour to Chinatown."

The driver glanced at his boss in the rearview mirror. Their eyes met. Understood.

High Plains' Hop Alley had sprung up down in the bottom land, near the railroad tracks, back in the 1870's. A past governor, Ed McCook, had actually invited the Chinese to the territory, back when California was trying to get rid of the bastards. Back then, that land was good for nothing, and the immigrants made use of it. Built their laundries, their grub joints, pot houses, and opium dens, lived in the backrooms. But the land was worth a fortune these days and the handwriting was on the wall for little family-run businesses. Ratzer knew his days of squeezing the Chinese were coming to an end, so he would squeeze 'em all a little harder today. One by one, he stopped at their places of business. They all knew what he was there for.

"Mister Sheriff, good to see you," Sing Li said with false deference. His Oriental Saloon, Pool Hall, and Restaurant was the most ambitious of Chinatown's establishments. "What can I do for you?" Unlike his neighbors, Mr. Sing would make Ratzer ask outright.

"I'll have the usual."

"You mean, Peking Duck?"

"I mean the cash." The sheriff sat at the nearest table, waiting for the protection money to be brought to him in a to-go bag. A mélange of smells, of oil and spices and garlic wafted from the kitchen. Ratzer realized he was hungry. Actually, Ratzer would have hated to shut the Oriental down. This was his favorite restaurant in town. Mr. Sing's Peking Duck was to die for, made fresh daily from fowl raised in the city's parks, caught after dark, and served up with a variety of savory side dishes, a gastronomic wonder. And while you were waiting for the food to be prepared, there was the massage parlor next door. That little China doll had such skillful hands. But not today. That grippe, that damned germ whose ass he kicked, had left him feeling tired, nonetheless. He was afraid his main man muscle might not rear its ugly head. Had that nurse managed to sabotage him? Had she slipped him a mickey? Switched out his blue pill for some other little blue pill?

Mr. Sing brought him a bag of hundos, on top of which was a white take-out carton of his famous dish. "Thank you, Mister Sheriff, for your protection."

Ratzer nodded his accord and took his leave. From the back alley, the sound of gunfire. Ratzer pretended not to hear. It might have been a gentlemen's duel; it might have been drunk cowboys. Maybe even Chinese fireworks. In any case, he had people to take care of that. Couldn't risk any confrontations himself. As sheriff, he had friends in high places, but he had enemies in low places. He worked hard for the kickbacks, the bribes, the skimming. But he didn't want to be a law enforcer forever. For him, the office was a steppingstone to the Big House on Fourteenth Avenue. Bully Ratzer wasn't just any old body wearing a star. To ensure his reputation stayed clean, Ratzer had called on a rogue gunman to finish off Nurse Kit Carson.

Things were heating up, for a Tuesday night. The smell of burning incense, of opium, of joss paper – hell money – for the ancestors. Everywhere in Chinatown, red paper lanterns and the pop- pop- pop of firecrackers in the alleys. This was the night of the hungry ghost festival, or some such voodoo these superstitious Chinks celebrated. On top of that, you had your drunk Micks and Spicks trying to fight them, each other, and every other damn body in sight. Hell, let 'em. Li had delivered a bag of silver and Bully Ratzer had beat the grippe. Now his belly was full. Life was good again.

Then, a text from his best deputy: *Local forecast - Balmy Wether back in town.*

What, that little half- breed bitch was back? Now what in hell did she want? No

good could come of that, not with the election coming up. He would have her picked

up and driven out to the eastern badlands. Or at least as far as East Colfax. In any

case, he needed to leave before the shooting got out of hand.

Balmy

They walked together, through the camps, toward Chinatown. High Plains did not

hold good memories for her. She had lived and worked at the O.K. Corral

Gentlemen's Club for as long as she could remember. Which wasn't really that far

back. Something bad must've happened to her to cause her early memory

repression. She had heard somewhere that the subconscious remembers

everything – every image, every word, every feeling. But she remembered enough

bad shit to bring down Bully Ratzer.

A bottle rocket whistled, a flash of light, over the rooftops of the carryout

liquor stores, car rentals, immigrant grocery stores. A billboard – WELLMART'S

HEALTHCARE HEROES SAVE LIVES – a bold banner above a team of masked

employees wearing red, white, and blue spangled capes, their arms crossed like

badasses. An orange- haired woman riding a wheelchair crossed the street, coming

toward them, yelling, "Hey, kids, any utes got a smoke?" At least that sounded like what she said. But they were not Utes and no, they did not. They did not smoke.

The woman cursed them and rolled away. The three walked on, falling in step.

The sound of gunfire, or maybe it was backfire, somebody's muffler. A Mercedes wagon slowed, like it was following them. Black, with tinted windows, impossible to see through. Was she being paranoid? Those luxury sport utility vehicles were common in High Plains. Or was it Ratzer's posse? The directions on her phone showed they were nearly at the rendezvous point with the reporter. Had they been tracking her through her phone all along?

Pancho Villa

Oscar Ramirez (a.k.a. Pancho Villa, the avatar on his I.D. badge) was Wellmart's Employee of the Month. His reward was to have his photograph on the wall in the hall of fame leading to the parking garage. He also got to wear a badge; a gold star made of aluminum. Although he did not give a damn about the award, he wore the badge on the pocket of his scrubs. He wore it because it entitled him to one free meal every shift he worked, all month long. It also entitled him to use the complementary Employee of the Month parking spot. Pancho rode a bicycle to work. He chained it to the metal post holding the sign that said Employee of the Month. He had a vehicle, a Bronco, but he had gotten popped with a DUI a few months ago and the sheriff had taken his license. He had not even been behind the wheel, but asleep on his couch. An anonymous caller had turned him in. Ratzer had shown up at his apartment and made a deal. Your license for six months, and a hundo for "processing fees". When Pancho showed up at the Sheriff's office six months and one day later, the clerk had no record of the charge and no license to return. Pancho was still mounted on two wheels, instead of four. But he felt better than he had for a long time.

Pancho had survived the cost containment cuts the department had been forced to implement. He was reliable, thorough, and had a friendly manner. Like most employees of the month, he went the extra mile. What that meant in corporate terms was that he worked overtime without pay, did tasks outside his job description, when asked, and made other people look good. Employee of the Month was the ultimate attaboy given to make overworked people feel appreciated. But the parking spot and the free meal, that shit was real.

And then he was approached, he was invited, he was tapped by the doctor herself. Halliday wanted him to join the vigilantes for healthcare justice. Would he help smuggle a sick patient *out* of the hospital? Damn straight, he would. The only good thing he had to say about the hospital he worked for was that it was clean. You could practically eat off the floor. And if the nurses were messy, leaving used IV tubing hanging after patient discharge, dripping its last few drops onto his clean, practically sterile floor, if the trashcans sometimes contained hazardous waste, it was because there were not enough of them. They were responsible for too many patients, all of them too sick, too injured, to take care of themselves. That was why they were in the hospital, not for a holiday, a spa treatment. The administrators did not take care of the patients, draw their blood, did not start their IVs, did not deliver their chemotherapy, did not change their bloody dressings, or empty their urinals, their urine bags, their bedpans, nor did they change their sweaty sheets, monitor their vital signs, or give them their medications. The doctors did not do any of that either. It was the nurses who did that. And it was the people in his department – Environmental Services – who kept the place properly sanitized. A hospital is not a healing place if it is not clean, orderly, and safe.

As Pancho dressed and gunned up for work that day, he felt a sense of pride in his work, something he hadn't felt for a long while. He was a vigilante for healthcare justice, invited by Doc Halliday herself.

Doc Halliday

Before starting her shift at Wellmart Emergency, Doctor Ruth Halliday went upstairs to look in on Nurse Carson, who had a bad case of the grippe. Expecting to find her much improved and ready for discharge, Ruth was shocked to discover, almost by accident, Carson stuck in the linen supply closet at the end of the hall, forgotten, dehydrated, "HELP ME" scrawled on the pillowcase in what looked like her own blood. Talk about short-staffing – my God, this woman needed skilled, 'round the clock nursing care! If she was to have a chance in hell of surviving, she would have to be taken someplace where she could get the care she needed, and fast. Halliday was a doctor, but she had no jurisdiction up here, on the floors. She was an emergency medicine doc; her domain was downstairs in the fast lane.

Standing there helpless in the linen closet, Halladay texted Tonto, but the Indian was apparently still AWOL, on a vision quest. He was off the grid, might as well be dead himself. Hopefully, he'd check his messages soon. The vigilantes meant well but they were rogues, every damn one. Available when it suited them. She missed her military days. An order was an order. You couldn't pick and choose your assignment; you simply did what you were told.

"Kit?" The nurse opened her eyes when Halliday spoke her name. Responsive; that's a good sign. Stethoscope to ears, she listened to her lungs, which sounded like a 1953 washing machine. But she was young and had no underlying disease. What she needed was fluids, postural drainage, ambulation – in other words, good nursing care.

"Hang on, old girl. We're going to get you out of here."

Halliday left to find the charge nurse. There was none. Not a nurse to be found on the entire floor. In fact, there wasn't an employee to be seen. Halliday put in a call to the hospitalist, Doc Adams, and headed for the elevators. She would go to the top and speak with Boots Calhoun, the acting CEO. Only a miracle could save Kit Carson now. The elevator doors opened; out stepped three armed guards.

"Doctor Halliday," the biggest one said. "We're here to escort you off the property.

"What is this, a joke? I work here."

"Not anymore, you don't. Come with us, Halliday."

Their faces impassive, their tin stars gleaming, the guards ushered her down the hallway. She couldn't very well resist; she was outnumbered and outgunned.

"I need to use the restroom."

"Make it quick. And don't give us any trouble." He touched the handle of the handgun in plain view on his hip.

Inside the stall, Ruth pulled out her phone and put in the call. The new recruit from Environmental Services was their last ace. Halladay hoped he could carry out the plan alone.

"Is this Pancho Villa?"

"At your service, Doctor Halliday."

"I've got a favor to ask."

Wyatt

The reporter was sitting at the back of the saloon, hunched over a plate of Chinese dumplings. Wyatt thought he recognized her from the news channel Abuela watched every evening. Polly Pry, that was her name. Big dark eyebrows and fake, plump lips.

"That's her," Balmy said with a little tremor of excitement. "That's Polly Pry. You boys wait for me outside, OK?"

"But –"

He felt a rip of pain, watching her walk toward the back of the saloon. She thought he was just a kid, and he longed to prove her wrong. To show her how capable he was. How understanding of whatever it was she needed to tell the reporter. And the truth was, he was hungry. The food smelled good.

"Come on," said Mike, nudging him in the side. "Let's go watch billiards."

Reluctantly he followed Mike toward the smack of pool balls from the adjoining room. Looking over his shoulder, he saw Balmy pull up a stool and sit across the table from the reporter. The way she straddled it, like she was riding a horse. Their heads were together, already connecting, deep in conversation.

Some serious pool shooting back at the tables. Men who knew what they were doing. Wasn't much drinking going on, not back here in the billiard room. That's how you can tell it's serious, Mike said. Serious players don't drink much. They watched a while, then got restless. More fun to play than to watch.

"Hey, Chica, I didn't know you worked here." Mike, following a young waitress back into the kitchen. Mike seemed to know a lot of people, way more than he did. Wyatt followed Mike who cajoled the waitress, hinting for a handout, an eggroll maybe, or a fortune cookie. But just then Mr. Sing appeared and scolded them. "Get on home, young fellas."

"We're looking for Zhang," Wyatt said, thinking fast.

"He's got work to do. No time for loitering."

Wyatt envied Zhang his employment. He wished he had a paying job. Then he would have some money to play pool, he'd have money to wager. Money to buy something to eat.

The two boys went back into the saloon just in time to see Balmy walking toward the exit, in between two figures, one male and one female. It looked like she was being escorted out. But the female was not the reporter. The reporter was nowhere to be seen. Wyatt darted toward them.

"Hey, Mister!" Wyatt called out loudly, to be heard above the bar noise. He didn't dare call out Balmy's name. The man, who had hold of Balmy's elbow with his right hand, turned to look at him, and as he did, he revealed the pistol in his left hand, aimed at her ribcage. Now shit started happening real fast, so fast that Wyatt didn't stop to think but pulled out his own pistol, puny in comparison to the guy's nine-millimeter, but Wyatt's hand was fast. At that very moment, the gun was part of his hand, like his joystick. He and the antique Smith & Wesson seven shooter were one. The room became a video screen, his gaze was wide, he saw everything. He saw and he reacted, squeezing the trigger, seeing the surprise on the man's face as he fell, feeling the kick against his palm, the sting, saw his hand jerk. Joysticks don't jerk. This was real. Balmy lurched, but the bitch cop coldcocked her with the butt of her gun, then turned it on Wyatt, but he was already firing. And again, he watched the bitch cop go down, her piece firing as it hit the saloon floor. Now the other customers were drawing their weapons and scrambling for cover wherever they could. Another shot rang out – it was not from his piece – and another, from the far side of the room. The sound of breaking glass, a woman's scream, and Merle Haggard singing "I think I'll just stay here and drink."

Suddenly, there was Mike, pulling Balmy away, pulling her by the legs across the saloon floor. Wyatt squeezed the trigger again, and the gun blew up in his hand. But his target was hit, the other cop was down. The saloon erupted in a brawl, the sound of cursing, glass breaking, everyone was fighting, it was a real barroom blitz. Someone grabbed his arm, it was Zhang.

"Come with me!"

Wyatt followed him to the billiard room where Mike had dragged Balmy under a pool table. Her eyes had opened, she was coming to consciousness.

"I've got a place you can hide," Zhang said. Supporting a dazed Balmy between them, they followed him to a liquor storage room where he locked them inside. "I'll come get you when it's safe."

"Dude!" said Mike to Wyatt.

"What?"

"Your hand. Are you OK?"

Wyatt still gripped the antique pistol, or what was left of it. But his hand was black with third degree burns, and parts of the gun appeared to be melted. Later, it would hurt like a sumbitch but right now he felt nothing but elation. They had saved Balmy from Ratzer's men.

Kit Carson

Doctors all but disappear when there is no longer a viable cure. They may write the orders for a compassionate extubation, or for compassionate amounts of morphine or hydromorphone, but those fuckers seldom stick around for the person's passing. So that explains why there were no doctors, but there were no nurses either. Maybe I am already dead? If so, purgatory was a linen closet, because that's where I seem to be, crammed between two stainless steel carts of blankets, sheets, and pillowcases.

No, wait, I can't be dead. I have kids to raise, lives to save, and a man's heart to win. This is no country for old nurses. *Don't give up yet, Kit. Gather your strength. Sleep and dream.* Dreams, like short, surreal film clips, unfolding on the screen behind my eyes.

The rumble, the song of his motorcycle – blocks away. I see him in the saddle, hair the color of steel, the hard curve of a bare arm. He stops for me and I climb on behind, though I cannot, for the life of me, remember his name. I cling to him as the machine flies, my face buried in his neck, his hair tickling my lips, my hands on his hips. I don't know where we're going but we're moving, I don't care where. I've never been happier than now. In this multisensory dream movie, the air is filled with green smells, just-cut hay, cottonwood seeds. Layers of coolness, layers of smells. Jump cut to motorcycle resting on its kickstand, he and I scrambling up an embankment to lie in the grass and pine needles. Wilson's Peak in the distance, endless blue above. He devours me. I can see his single tattoo, feel the scar on the skin covering his left flank, his latissimus dorsi. I trace it with my fingers, memorizing his back with my hands. Breathing in his sighs. Breathing out my own. The breeze whispers in the aspen leaves. This, this is Valhalla, this is The Big Valley in the sky. Below, I see my tombstone:

Here lies Kit Carson, Mother and Nurse,

She lived and she died

To pad the Corporation's purse

But wait, that's not how I want to die. No, it's all wrong. Stop the film, the video, whatever is playing. Press Pause, something's wrong. It can't end like this. But I can't press the pause button, I can't press the call button, there is no call button, and I can't seem to move at all. I'm back inside my head, I feel my heart pounding, I'm gasping for air. Outside my door, a tall figure, backlit, a silhouette. I'm afraid it is Death, come for me.

Pancho Villa

Standing at the foot of her bed, the nurse looked as lifeless as a dry leaf. He turned off the monitor alarms, disconnected the IV – it looked like it ran dry days ago – then scooped her body into his arms as if she were his dead bride, or maybe his child. Then, aware of someone standing just outside the door, he placed her warm body onto the cart – a covered cadaver carrier, the special gurney used to transport dead bodies, unseen, through hospital corridors. He pulled over the cover, placed a sheet and pillow on the top for the ruse. Out of the linen closet, looking past the stranger carrying a rifle, standing outside the door, down the long corridor to the service elevator. Press B for basement. Down here, the low hum, the slow heartbeat of the hospital, could be heard, it could be felt, an electrical vibration, rolling past the electrical room – RESTRICTED – the Engineering room – KEEP OUT – through the delivery door and into the waiting mortuary van where a team of first responders – vigilante paramedics and EMTs – worked hard to rehydrate and oxygenate Kit. The driver, a champion bull rider, drove like the wind to the old fort on the edge of High Plains where Tonto had set up a field hospital. From here, she would be transported under cover to her own home where she would either recover to fight another day or pass on to the next world.

In any case, Pancho's work here was done. For today. But now that he had a taste of vigilante healthcare, he was ready for more.

Lone Gunman

Willie walked down the corridor, his spurs ringing with each step. The rooms were occupied but the hallway was empty. He paused before the door at the end of the hallway, the closet where his victim was being housed, and watched as the orderly pushed the cadaver cart out. The gunman touched the brim of his hat in respect. He knew a cadaver cart when he saw one. Sure enough, the nurse's bed was empty. An IV infusion pump, standing at attention, but turned off. The plastic tubing, just removed, looped like a lariat on the floor. The name on the plastic bag of antibiotics confirmed it: Carson, Kit. Looks like Death's angel had beat him to it. He heard the ping of the elevator, the swoosh of the doors opening. There goes the body, off to the morgue.

Now that he was here, might as well earn his money. See if some other poor sonofabitch needed to be put out of their misery. From the supply cart he took a protective paper gown, hat, gloves, and mask. He covered his cowboy boots with blue paper slippers. Then, carefully wrapping another blue isolation gown around his thirty-aught-six, he rode the elevator up to the Intensive Care Unit to do a little side job. But someone had beat him to it. Richard Beamis was dead, his alarms ringing like a Wyoming wind chime, the tracing of his heart's electrical activity a line as flat as Kansas. From his bedside, a nursette looked up, a large syringe in hand, equipped with an 18-gauge needle.

"Help you?"

"I'm looking for Richard Beamis."

"Sorry, sir, he just drew his last breath."

Well, hell's bells, imagine that. Was the Grim Reaper furloughing him? Or maybe just limiting his practice to outside the hospital's walls.

Boots Calhoun

From her penthouse office, behind the heirloom mahogany desk that had belonged to Big Dick Beamis's robber baron grandfather, Wellmart's new CEO spoke to the reporter on the phone, in an official statement. The founder and former CEO had died of complications following a cerebral vascular accident – a stroke. She ended the call, quite pleased with herself. Actually, a bolus of air injected into his bloodstream by a nursette was what had killed him, but it is quite common for stroke victims to encounter second strokes in the first days and weeks following the initial ischemic attack. There was no reason to suspect anything else, no autopsy would be performed. His widow would get his pension and a sizeable life insurance payout, but she was not part of the company structure, she was not on the board of directors. Even if she questioned her husband's death and requested an autopsy, in High Plains the coroner was the sheriff. Calhoun then wrote out a sizable check to Bully Ratzer's gubernatorial campaign from Friends of American Healthcare, LLC.

Despite the breaking news implicating Sheriff Bully Ratzer in a sex trafficking scheme, no arrests were made. Ratzer continued to dominate in the polls. The people of High Plains didn't give the accusation much thought. Right now, the grippe was the hot topic. The story of Ratzer kicking the grippe's ass had more coverage than allegations about his supposed involvement in the sexual exploitation and prostitution of minors. This was, after all, the Wild West.

In Beamis's memory, Boots Calhoun poured herself a shot of his good whiskey and picked a Cubano from his private humidor, now that she held the keys. She licked that cigar, clipped it, and with a lighter from her own purse, lit it, gently sucking, her surgically tightened cheeks puffing, puffing, puffing. She knew what the hell she was doing. Kicking back in Beamis's ergonomic office chair, she put her bespoke snakeskin cowboy boots on the desktop and enjoyed a quiet moment of celebration.

Kit Carson

The crisp, smoky scent of burning sage. Wake up! Familiar voices, like birds chirping. Open my eyes to see their faces, a wreath around me, my family gathered around the deathbed, my deathbed. Not a hospital bed, but my very own queen size, PosturePerfect mattress, covered by my own saddle blanket. There's no place like home to die. Surrounded by my loved ones, attended by the best and sexiest nurse ever. I am still breathing, my heart is beating, and I realize I am hungry. He helps me sit up, and Grandmother brings me chicken soup. He holds the spoon, I sip the broth. Green chili bites my tongue, opens my nostrils. I am alive, I want to live.

*

We held the funeral that Tuesday, a small gathering of family and friends in the living room. The rosewood box on a pedestal, a wreath of tumbleweeds and prairie sage, a ribbon that proclaimed BELOVED MOTHER. Next to it, a photograph of Kit Carson in her prime, dressed in blue scrubs, edited with a pair of angel wings coming out of her back. Abuela, uncles, Mike – the Trujillos all dressed in their best, and my son Wyatt, cowboy hat in hand, a hand wrapped in white gauze from a burn, I was told. (Later, he would confess the whole truth, how he shot the deputy, then the next round misfired, burning his hand.) Beside him, Calamity,

45

dressed in a white linen frock, her hair braided by Abuela's experienced hands and wrapped around her head like a renaissance crown. In her clenched fist, a bouquet of my favorite yellow wildflowers. Tough little weeds, dandelions. So restorative, their bitter young leaves.

A phalanx of healthcare vigilantes, stethoscopes looped like lariats around their necks, stood at attention in front of the woodstove. With ceremonial precision, Doc Halliday and Pancho Villa folded the white silk banner, upon which was printed HEALTHCARE HERO, which Doc herself presented to Wyatt, with a solemn salute. Tears welled in my eyes and slid down my cheeks. Tonto got up to speak, after which he passed the hat for The Caring Ranch, a nonprofit co-op hospital managed by nurses. Our mission statement: Let none who enter pay more than they can afford. Halliday advised me to choose a new alias, as Kit Carson was dead. That would take some thought. At that moment I was content to be nameless, newly born.

That night, by the light of the midsummer full moon, we made a campfire out back and buried the rosewood box beneath the cottonwood tree. On top of the mound of freshly dug earth, Calamity planted a popsicle stick cross on which she had printed R.I.P. HAMMIE. We sang Happy Trails to You and Tim, who had ditched the moniker Tonto, recited an Arapaho story about animal spirits, opened a bottle of whiskey to celebrate, and passed it around. Later, Zhang delivered Mr. Sing's Peking Duck, sixteen side dishes, and complementary fortune cookies all packaged in white take-out boxes. At midnight, Abuela served her pan de Muertos (bread of the dead) fresh out of the oven, to everyone's delight. As intended, the Mexican funeral food replenished my spirit as well as my body.

Later, when the guests had gone and the family was asleep, Tim and I sat outside under the stars, watching the logs turn red. He brought out his pipe and we smoked a bowl of a native weed believed to have curative properties.

"Kiss me, Kemosabe."

Our lips pressed together, we inhaled each other's breath, and somewhere deep within I felt the dry kindling of my libido reignite. Tim knew just what to do. He blew gently on the sparks, and before long we had a hot campfire blazing, a fire that lasted until dawn. Old night shift nurses like us, we are used to caring for others while the rest of the world sleeps. That Tuesday night, it was our own lives we were saving.

*****

Nurse Kit Carson's Knife & Gun Club

A rodeo of short stories by L.S. Collison

available in electronic format, collectible paperbacks, and audio format

Friday Night Knife & Gun Club

Saturday Night Knife & Gun Club

Sunday Night Knife & Gun Club

Monday Night Knife & Gun Club

Tuesday Night Requiem

author photo - PhotoZ by Sheila. Sheila Zappanti

Cover art by Gregory Block; cover design by M.G. Manelis

Also by L.S. Collison:

Holiday on Planet Jolieterre; a Nova Skylar Space Nurse Adventure
(2014)

www.fictionhouseltd.com

www.lindacollison.com